For Leo

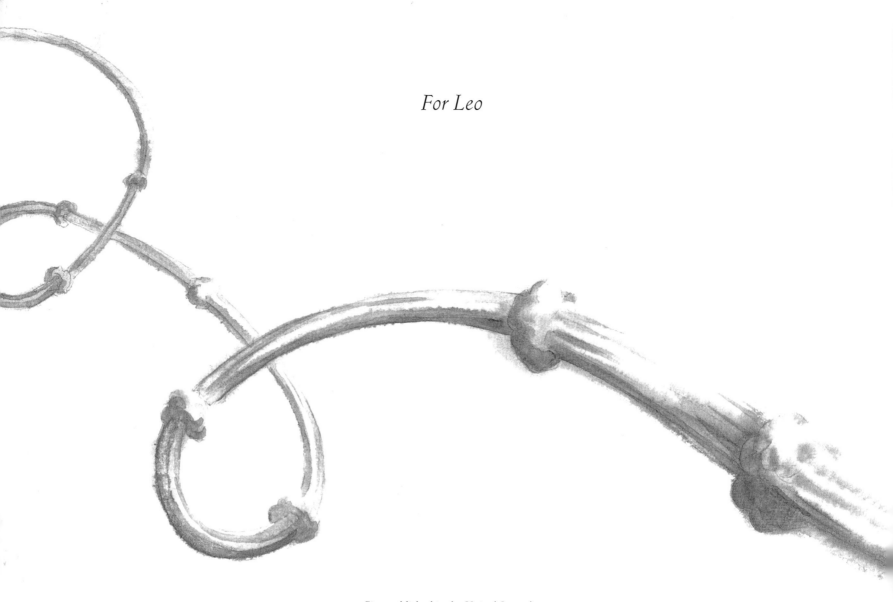

First published in the United States by
Dial Books for Young Readers
A division of Penguin Young Readers Group
345 Hudson Street
New York, New York 10014

Published in Great Britain
by Frances Lincoln Limited
Copyright © 2004 by M. P. Robertson
All rights reserved
Manufactured in Singapore
3 5 7 9 10 8 6 4 2

Library of Congress Cataloging-in-Publication Data
Robertson, M. P.
The great dragon rescue / by M. P. Robertson.
p. cm.
Summary: George and his old friend the dragon try to
rescue a baby dragon from a witch.
ISBN 0-8037-2973-1
[1. Dragons–Fiction. 2. Witches–Fiction.] I. Title.
PZ7.R54843Gr 2004
[E]–dc21

The Great
DRAGON RESCUE

M. P. Robertson

DIAL BOOKS FOR YOUNG READERS
NEW YORK

Georege was bored one morning. When it came to fighting, chickens weren't half as brave as dragons.

While he gathered eggs from the chicken coop and daydreamed about *dragonish* things, he felt the coop shudder. Cautiously, he peeked his head out the door, and saw...

It was his old friend the dragon! Up, up they soared, George, the dragon, and the chicken coop. George shouted hello, but the dragon seemed anxious to get somewhere. They flew faster and faster until they came to a land where everything began with *Once upon a time*.

They dropped down into a dark, dank forest.
The dragon led George through the trees until
they could see a flickering light ahead.

   From behind a tree they watched as a warty
witch barbecued toads on a dragon's flame.
The dragon was only a fledgling, barely out
of the egg. It looked scared and sad. Then,
suddenly noticing George and the dragon, its
eyes opened wide and its tail began to wave.

George and the dragon stayed hidden until the witch had gobbled her way through a cauldron full of toads.

Soon they could hear her snores rattling the windows of the cottage.

George rushed to open the cage, but as he struggled with the knot, the witch's crow flapped around the cage, squawking, "WAKE UP–WAKE UP, WITCH! Someone's stealing the dragon."

The witch came bursting out, her wand crackling with spells.

"Who dares to steal my barbecue?" she roared.

Now, George had read enough fairy tales to know that witches are very boastful.

"I don't believe you are a witch," he said. "Real witches can fly on broomsticks."

"Of course I'm a witch! I'm the quickest, wickedest witch in the west," she bragged.

"My dragon has beaten the wicked witches of the north, south, and east," George fibbed. "I bet he can beat you too!"

"I bet he can't," sneered the witch. "Let's race around the enchanted castle and back. When I win, I'll turn you both into toads for my supper!"

She jumped on her broomstick. "On yer marks. Get set . . ." And she was gone.

The witch was frighteningly fast.

But the dragon was faster.

Soon the witch and the dragon were neck and neck.

As the enchanted castle came into view, the dragon was in the lead. George looked back to see the witch weaving a spell.

But George had prepared a secret weapon. Just before the spell was cast, he pelted the witch with eggs.

The witch was in a terrible rage. There was a blinding flash–but the egg that dripped from her wand had scrambled the spell.

Back they flew to the witch's house. But by the
time they landed on the roof, all that remained of
the witch was her broomstick and her hat.

Cautiously, George lifted the hat. Hidden beneath
was a large, smelly, warty toad.

It will be a hundred years before a prince
kisses that! he thought.

Then he set the baby dragon free. It ran to the big dragon with a roar of delight.

George didn't speak Dragon, but he knew exactly what the baby had said . . .
"*Daddy.*"

It was time for George to return home. The
chickens would be missing their coop, and
his parents would be missing George.

Up, up they soared, and George waved good-bye to
the land where everything ended with *happily ever after.*
Unless you're a witch . . . or a toad!